TALK OF THE TAPE

By the time Tina raced to the track, the crowd around Alex had grown quite large.

"I was tripped," Alex growled. "Otherwise I would have won."

"Don't be a sore loser, Alex," Tommy Choi called out. He had walked back from the finish line. His face was red from running.

Suddenly Tina gasped. "The camera!" She ran back to the bench where she had left it. There was a long smear of red paint on it, near the tape slot. And then Tina noticed the most important thing of all: The videotape from the camera was missing.

Tina carried the camera over to her friends. Alex was still trying to convince them that he had been tripped.

"I know you were tripped," Tina told him. She held up the camera. "Someone stole the tape of the race."

"Hey! There's only one reason that I can think of why someone would take the tape."

"Yeah!" Lenni said. "It must show who tripped you."

Join the Team!

Do you watch GHOSTWRITER on PBS? Then you know that when you read and write to solve a mystery or unravel a puzzle, you're using the same smarts and skills the Ghostwriter team uses.

We hope you'll join the team and read along to help solve the mysterious and puzzling goings-on in these GHOSTWRITER books!

Courting Danger

and

Other Stories

by
Dina Anastasio

Illustrated by Eric Velasquez

A
**CHILDREN'S TELEVISION WORKSHOP
BOOK**

BANTAM BOOKS
NEW YORK • TORONTO • LONDON • SYDNEY • AUCKLAND

COURTING DANGER AND OTHER STORIES
A Bantam Book / November 1992

Ghostwriter **Gh st** writer and ● are
trademarks of Children's Television Workshop.
All rights reserved. Used under authorization.

Art direction by Marva Martin
Cover design by Susan Herr
Interior illustrations by Eric Velasquez

ISBN 0-553-48070-7

Published simultaneously in the United States and Canada

Bantam Books are published by Bantam Books, a division of Bantam
Doubleday Dell Publishing Group, Inc. Its trademark, consisting of the
words "Bantam Books" and the portrayal of a rooster, is Registered in
U.S. Patent and Trademark Office and in other countries. Marca Reg-
istrada. Bantam Books, 666 Fifth Avenue, New York, New York 10103.

PRINTED IN THE UNITED STATES OF AMERICA

OPM   0 9 8 7 6 5 4 3

Contents

Photo Finish

Nine-year-old Gaby Fernandez cleared her throat and raised her microphone.

"Welcome to the Fort Greene Community Center Race," she said. "It's a beautiful spring day here in the park. The sun is shining. There are twelve different species of birds in the trees. We're all here to raise money for the community center, and we're all here to watch the race."

"You said that twice," Tina Nguyen whispered. She focused her camera and zoomed in on the runners poised at the starting line.

"Said what?" Gaby asked.

"We're all here. You said 'we're all here' two times."

"That's the way I talk," Gaby said, lowering the

microphone. "A reporter has to develop a style, doesn't she? Well, maybe my style will be that I say some things twice. You know—"

"Quiet, Gaby!" Tina interrupted. "The runners are about to begin."

"Okay, okay." Gaby rolled her eyes. But really, she didn't mind so much when Tina bossed her around. After all, Tina was a year older than she was. Tina was also the producer of the school news video. She knew a lot about making TV shows. Gaby planned to be a reporter for one of the big stations someday. Tina was helping her with her career.

When Tina gave the signal, Gaby raised the microphone again and went on.

"They're off," she said. "It's Tommy Choi in the lead, and here comes Alex Fernandez, my big brother. . . ."

"Don't say he's your brother," Tina whispered.

"Here comes Alex Fernandez," Gaby repeated. "He's on the outside of the track. Looking good, Alex! Go, Alex!"

Gaby was about to cheer some more. Then she caught Tina's glare. She smiled guiltily and continued.

"And coming on strong is Katherine Brown . . . she's passing Henry Livingston, and now she's passing Tommy, and Alex . . . As they head toward the finish line, it's Alex and Tommy and Katherine . . . no, it's Henry, no . . ."

Suddenly Gaby fell silent.

Tina nudged her. "What's the matter?" she asked.

"It's Alex. Something's the matter with Alex."

Tina zoomed in on Alex's dark brown hair and determined face. Gaby was right. Alex was stumbling. He was trying to get his footing. Now he was falling forward. "I think he's hurt," Tina shouted.

Gaby shoved the microphone into Tina's hand and raced across the grass. Alex's friends, Jamal Jenkins and Lenni Frazier, were right behind her. Other people followed them. By the time Tina had carefully placed her camera and the microphone on a red bench and raced over to the track, the crowd around Alex had grown quite large. Not many people noticed that Tommy Choi had come in first.

"It's not too bad," Gaby said, as Tina pushed her way through the crowd. "He just skinned his knee."

"I didn't *just* skin my knee," Alex growled. He looked furious. "I was tripped. Otherwise I would have won."

"Don't be a sore loser, Alex," Tommy Choi called out. He had walked back from the finish line. His face was red from running.

Jamal and Lenni looked at each other. Could Tommy be right? Was Alex just being a sore loser?

Suddenly Tina gasped. "The camera!" She ran back to the bench where she had left it, hoping no one had stolen it.

The microphone and the camera were still there. But when Tina picked up the camera she noticed something. There was a long smear of red paint on it, near the tape slot.

Tina looked at her fingers. They were red too. When she looked back at the bench, she spotted a small sign that she hadn't noticed before. WET PAINT, it said.

"Oh, great," Tina said. Now there was paint all over the Washington Elementary School's camera and microphone!

And then Tina noticed the most important thing of all: The videotape from the camera was missing.

Tina carried the camera and the microphone over to her friends. Alex was still trying to convince them that he had been tripped.

"You've gotta believe me," he was saying. "I *know* I was tripped."

"I know you were tripped too," Tina told him. She held up the camera and pointed to the smear of red paint. "Someone stole the tape of the race," she said.

"Hey! There's only one reason that I can think of why someone would take the tape," Alex said. "Because that tape proves that I was tripped." He was so excited that his words came out in double time.

"Yeah!" Lenni said. "It must show who tripped you."

Tina held up her red fingers. "More evidence," she

said. "There's paint all around the tape slot on the camera. Whoever took the film must have red fingers too."

"So to find out who tripped Alex, we have to find someone with red fingers," Jamal said.

Tina nodded. "That's just what I'm going to do. I'm going to catch him—or her—red-handed!" Turning, she ran off to the winner's circle.

"Having red paint on your hands doesn't prove you're guilty," Lenni said suddenly. "It's suspicious, but it's not complete proof."

"Oh, yeah." Jamal frowned and poked at the ground with his sneaker. Then he looked up. "We need some *other* way to prove who did it. We need a backup plan."

"Think, Alex," Gaby urged. "Try to remember something, anything, about the person who tripped you."

Alex wrinkled his forehead. "I remember that he, or she, was wearing a blue T-shirt," he said slowly. "And there were letters on the T-shirt. I definitely remember a *D*, and maybe an *O*. I remember thinking that the letters made me think of a deer."

Gaby pulled a small notebook and a pencil out of her pocket. In capital letters she wrote down:

EVIDENCE

1. PERSON WHO TRIPPED ALEX WORE BLUE T-SHIRT.

2. T-SHIRT HAD LETTERS ON IT. ONE WAS D. THE OTHER MIGHT HAVE BEEN O. LETTERS MADE ALEX THINK OF DEER.

3. PERSON WHO TOOK VIDEOTAPE HAS RED PAINT ON FINGERS.

"Whoa! Look!" Jamal pointed excitedly at the page in Gaby's notebook. Suddenly some of the letters she had written began to jump around on the page. An *I* left its place in the word *tripped*. Then the *S* from *person* leaped down to join the *I*. In no time at all a new sentence had formed at the bottom of the page. It read: IS ALEX ALL RIGHT?

Jamal looked at Alex, then at Lenni, then at Gaby.

"Ghostwriter," they all whispered at the same time.

Ghostwriter was a ghost who had begun to talk to

Jamal through his computer one day. Soon the ghost had contacted Lenni, Alex, and Gaby too. That was the start of the Ghostwriter team.

None of the team knew exactly who Ghostwriter was or where he had come from. What they did know was that Ghostwriter was a good friend. Though he couldn't talk to the team, he could write to them. And even though he couldn't hear, he could read anything, anywhere. That was very useful when there was a mystery to be solved.

"Ghostwriter's here! Cool!" Gaby said. "I'm going to tell him how Alex fell and nearly broke his neck." She started to scribble in her notebook.

"Give me that," Alex said. He grabbed the pencil and pad from Gaby and wrote, "I'M FINE, GHOST-WRITER. BUT I WANT TO FIND OUT WHO TRIPPED ME."

"Hey," Lenni said. "I just thought of something. All of the runners who were close to Alex when he tripped were wearing blue T-shirts. I remember no-ticing that."

"Maybe Ghostwriter can narrow it down," Jamal said. He quickly asked Ghostwriter to find the writing on the T-shirts.

A minute later the letters on Gaby's notepad began moving, as Ghostwriter responded.

T-SHIRT #1: MARTELLO'S DOES
            MEATBALLS LIKE MOM

T-SHIRT # 2: DOCTOR DEMENTO

T-SHIRT # 3: DEARBORNE STREET
            SCHOOL

"Got it!" Lenni cried. "*Dear*borne Street School. See, there's our *deer*. That's it. Case closed. All we have to do now is find the person in that T-shirt."

The team was about to head for the finish line and face the guilty person when the letters in one of the other two T-shirt slogans on the notepad began to glow.

"Ghostwriter!" Jamal said. "He's trying to tell us something else."

"Man, this whole page is jumping," Lenni said. "Oh, I see!" She pointed. "Those letters right there spell another word that could have made Alex think of a deer."

"Hey, that's right!" Alex cried.

Gaby's face fell. "I guess this case isn't closed yet," she said. "Unless Tina found out something."

Just then Tina ran up. She pushed her black bangs out of her eyes. "Guess what?" she asked. "*Two* of the runners have red paint on their hands. So now what do we do?"

"Two people with red hands. Two 'deer' T-shirts." Alex shook his head. "Beats me."

Suddenly Jamal grinned. "I know. We just put two and two together," he announced.

"Huh?" Gaby said. Then a grin spread across her face too. "Yeah, you're right!"

"I don't get it," Lenni said, looking puzzled.

"What's written on the T-shirts of the two people who have red paint on their hands?" Jamal asked Tina.

"I didn't notice," Tina said.

"It's time to find out," Gaby declared.

The team ran up to the winner's circle. Tommy, Henry, and Katherine were accepting their ribbons. Slowly the team walked past the three winners and gave each of them a high-five. As they did, they studied the runners' fingers. Tommy and Henry had red fingers.

When they were finished, they stood back and inspected the three front-runners' T-shirts. There was a green stain on Tommy's Dr. Demento T-shirt.

After a pause Jamal poked Gaby. "I think I've got it," he whispered.

Gaby nodded. "Me too."

"Me too," Lenni said. She stepped forward. "Okay, we caught you red-handed," she said to one of the runners. "Give Tina back her tape and tell the judge how you tripped Alex."

The cheater said, "Who, me?" and tried to look innocent. But everyone could tell they had the guilty person. All the evidence proved it.

"Yes, you," Jamal said. "That ribbon belongs to Alex. And next time keep your feet where they belong."

Who tripped Alex, and how did the team figure it out? If you think you know, write your answer on a separate piece of paper. If you need some help, solve the animal word search on page 12.

Courting Danger and Other Stories

Circle the words from the list below as you find them in the puzzle. Cross off every word you find on the list too. One word from the list is not in the puzzle. The leftover letters in the puzzle will tell you what that word means. Write the leftover letters onto the blanks below the puzzle. Then look for the word that's *not* in the word search on one of the T-shirts. Remember—the culprit has red hands *and* a T-shirt that reminded Alex of a deer.

* * *

WORD LIST:
boar   ewes   rams
buck   gander   rooster
bull   hens   sow
cow   mare   stallion
does

```
R A M S H E N S
O F B E B M A G
O S O W U L W A
S T A L L I O N
T E R D L E C D
E W E S M A R E
R B U C K E R R
```

Female Deer

Courting Danger

"**D**id you see that guy?" Lenni Frazier asked her father as they pushed through the crowd in front of Madison Square Garden. Max Frazier was taking Lenni and her friends on the Ghostwriter team to a New York Knicks basketball game.

"What guy?" Max asked.

"The guy selling tickets by the taxi stand."

"He wanted a hundred dollars for each ticket," Alex Fernandez said, shaking his head in amazement. "Did you pay a hundred dollars each for our tickets, Max?"

"For six tickets? Not!" Max said. "I ordered these tickets by mail. It was a special low-price offer."

Normally Max Frazier was a calm man. But the idea of paying $100 a ticket for a seat at a basketball game was too much. "I'm a musician," he reminded Alex. "Most musicians don't have hundred-dollar bills to toss around."

"I'll bet that guy gets his money," Jamal said. "Everybody wants a ticket to a Knicks game."

Max led Jamal, Alex, Gaby, Tina, and Lenni to the escalator and then down a corridor. When they reached their section doors Max handed the tickets to the ticket taker and put the ticket stubs into his pocket.

The lights inside the huge arena were almost blinding. Jamal gazed around. Madison Square Garden! A slow grin crept across his face as he took in the sights and sounds.

From far away he heard a man selling popcorn. "Get it while it's hot!" he called, shouting above the thumping pregame music. "Get your popcorn here!"

Knicks banners and signs were everywhere. They hung from the balconies. They waved above the heads of fans. They fluttered from the ceiling. And in the middle of the Garden, right above the basketball court, the scoreboard flashed:

Knicks Fever! Knicks Fever! Knicks Fever!

Max took the stubs out of his pocket and showed them to the Ghostwriter team. "I think we're here," he said.

"This is the right aisle," Tina said.

"Now we have to find our seats." Lenni took the stubs and led the way. Suddenly she stopped. Behind her the others stopped too. Lenni looked at their seats. She looked at the stubs in her hand. Then she looked back at the seats. "Uh-oh," she muttered.

All six seats were already taken.

"Excuse me," she said to the man on the aisle. "But I think you're in our seats."

"I don't think so," the man said. "We're in the right seats." He took three stubs out of his pocket, one for him and one for each of his daughters. He handed them to Lenni. Then the couple next to him took out their stubs. They passed them to Lenni and she compared them to the ones Max had given her.

The seat numbers on their tickets were the same as the numbers on the other tickets!

"As you can see," the man said firmly, "these seats belong to us." He sat down and folded his arms.

Lenni sighed. "I don't get it," she said. "Those tickets look just like ours."

"How could this happen?" Alex asked.

"I'm going to get an usher," Jamal announced. "I'll be right back."

He rushed up the aisle and waited while the usher talked to a small man in a suit. They seemed to be arguing, though Jamal couldn't hear what it was about. When the small man finally hurried away, Jamal led the usher down the aisle.

The usher was tall and skinny, with a bushy black mustache. "Forget it," he said when Max showed him their ticket stubs.

"Forget what?" Max asked.

The usher explained, "The seats. The game. You might as well head for home. Your tickets are fake. Half of the tickets in the Garden are fake tonight." The usher shrugged. "Sorry."

He didn't sound very sorry. He returned the stubs to Max and hurried back up the aisle.

"But what about the game?" Jamal cried.

"We're in the same boat," said a woman behind them. "Did you buy your tickets by mail?"

"That's right," Max admitted.

"So did we," the woman said. "So did an awful lot of people. And now there's a big problem. There are twice as many people here as there are seats!"

"I'm going to find someone in charge," Max said firmly. "There must be some way to straighten out this mess."

Jamal was disappointed. He and Alex walked down the aisle and gazed out at the court. Overhead, the scoreboard was lit up with a list of Rangers hockey games that were coming up. As they watched, the list scrolled down and new games appeared.

Dec. 12   Rangers vs. Flyers
Dec. 15   Dange s vs. Bruins
Dec. 20   Rangers vs. Oilers

The list was followed by: "Bewa e of pickpockets." Next, the words "Police R Watching!!" flashed on the screen.

Then the list of games popped back on the board.

"'Dange s'? 'Bewa e'? 'Police R Watching'?" Alex repeated. "Whoever is running that scoreboard needs to go back to school for spelling."

Jamal just nodded. He wasn't really listening. He was still thinking about the game.

"Hey, Jamal?" Alex said after a moment. "If Max got those tickets by mail, and many other people got their tickets from the same place, then it could be that that's where the fake tickets came from."

"I guess so," Jamal mumbled.

Above their heads the scoreboard flashed again. "Check it out," Alex whispered, grabbing Jamal's arm. "Ghostwriter's here!"

Jamal looked up. The letters on the scoreboard were settling into new words. Ghostwriter's message read:
REGARDS, FRIENDS!

"Hey!" Jamal cracked a grin. Knowing that Ghostwriter was there made him feel better.

As quickly as it had appeared, Ghostwriter's message vanished and was replaced by a new one. That one said:
AN ERROR? WHERE ARE THE RS?

Alex smiled. "Ghostwriter must be talking about how the *r* is missing in those words on the scoreboard."

Just then someone tapped Jamal on the shoulder. He turned around. It was Max, Lenni's father. Lenni, Tina, and Gaby stood behind him. Their faces were gloomy.

"There was nothing I could do," Max said. "In fact, the manager told me they were going to ask ticket-holders without seats to leave because of all the confusion. Come on, let's get out of here before we get caught in the crowd."

Jamal sighed. "This is beat," he said to Lenni. "We don't get to see the game, and I bet your dad won't get his money back, either."

"I know," Lenni agreed. "If only we could catch the jerks behind these fake tickets!"

"Yeah." Jamal nodded. "Maybe if we all brain-storm, we can come up with some way to find the crooks."

"We have to try at least," Lenni said. "You want to get together later today?"

"Yep. My house, five o'clock," Jamal said.

At that moment the tall, thin usher pushed past them, nearly knocking Gaby down.

"Hey, watch it!" Alex yelled. "That's my sister!"

The usher didn't stop. He raced up to the popcorn vendor, who was standing by the front row of seats. The usher said something. The popcorn vendor looked startled, then angry. He shook his head.

Behind the two men the scoreboard flashed:

Gaby burst out laughing. "That scoreboard's really weird," she said. "What kind of message is that?"

The usher stared at the strange sign for what seemed like a long time. Then he turned and ran for the doors.

The small man in the suit who had been talking to the usher earlier walked onto center court. "I'm Fred Zapinsky, manager here at the Garden. I'm sorry to say that we can't seat all of you," he said. "Those who don't have seats, please go home. Call the box office tomorrow. We'll refund your money or give you tickets to another event." His words boomed through the loudspeakers.

Max and the team didn't wait to hear the rest of his speech. They hurried out. No one said a word until they were back on the subway and heading toward home.

At five o'clock Gaby, Alex, and Lenni went over

to Jamal's house. Tina had to take care of her little sister, so she couldn't come.

The four kids borrowed Jamal's grandmother's small television and moved it into Jamal's room to watch the news. That was Gaby's idea. She thought they might pick up some facts that way. And she was right. The story about the tickets led the news.

"We've identified one of the suspects," a policewoman said. A picture of a man with a black mustache flashed across the screen.

"Hey!" Lenni cried. "That's our usher. See, he's got the same mustache."

Alex jumped up and leaned closer to the television. "Tall, thin, mean," he said. "That's him, all right."

"This isn't the first time fake tickets were sold for an event at the Garden," the police officer went on. "We've been looking into this for some time. We knew it was being run by someone at the arena. We were ready to close in on this fellow tonight. In fact, we tried to arrest him at the Garden, but he got away."

"He was in a hurry when he ran past us," Gaby said. "I bet he was making his getaway right then."

The officer continued. "Someone must have warned him that we were looking for him. We don't know who tipped him off or how. But we'll find out."

Jamal switched off the TV. "So now we know why that usher was in such a hurry," he said. "He knew the police were after him."

"I wonder how he knew," Lenni said.

"Maybe if we think of all the things that happened just before he ran away, we'll figure it out," Alex suggested.

"I'm going to take notes," Jamal said. He went over to his computer and turned it on. "That way Ghost-writer can join in if he has any ideas."

"Ghostwriter?" Gaby punched Alex in the arm. "Ghostwriter was at the Garden and you didn't tell the rest of us?"

"When was he there?" Lenni demanded. "What did he say? Why didn't you—"

"Give me a break!" Alex interrupted. "He was only there for a second or two. He just came to say hi."

"Yo!" Jamal called. Everyone looked at him. "Can we get back to business? What do we know about the usher?"

"He slouched," Gaby said immediately. "His mustache needed a trim. And—"

"Forget all that," Lenni told her. "Concentrate on the important stuff. Like did he talk to anyone?"

"The popcorn man," Gaby said. "They were arguing."

"And the manager," Jamal chimed in. "They were arguing too." His keyboard clicked as he typed.

Alex whistled. "Do you think one of them could have tipped him off?"

"Maybe," Lenni said. "But how can we know for sure?"

Jamal finished typing. He looked up and said, "Can

anybody think of anything else?"

"Hey. What about that screwy scoreboard?" Gaby said after a minute.

"Oh, that's right," Jamal said. He typed it in.

YES! Ghostwriter wrote back. MISSING R WAS VERY ODD.

Jamal frowned. "Hey, Alex, that's what you were talking about before. Remember, the scoreboard had all those missing *r*s."

"It was only missing an *r* sometimes," Alex said. "Like in the word *beware*."

Jamal began to type again.

"And don't forget that 'Rangers' was misspelled in one of the hockey game listings," Alex added.

"Right," Jamal said. "It was spelled 'Dangers.'" He typed that in.

Suddenly the letters on the screen flickered. NOT DANGERS, Ghostwriter wrote back. BE EXACT.

Gaby was reading over Jamal's shoulder. "Not dangers?" she asked. "What's that supposed to mean? Ask Ghostwriter."

"Uh-huh," Jamal said. His fingers flew over the keyboard.

NOT   DANGERS,   Ghostwriter   wrote. DANGE S.

"That's right." Lenni frowned. "Weird. The first *r* in 'Rangers' was changed to a *D*, and the second one was missing completely."

"*Very* weird," Jamal said. "Anybody who works

at Madison Square Garden should know how to spell Rangers."

"What a dumb mistake," Lenni said.

"Hey, wait," Alex said. "What if it wasn't a mistake at all?" He stared around at the rest of the team.

Jamal looked up. "You mean . . ."

"Yeah." Alex began to pace excitedly. "Look at the words that are missing the letter *r*. Beware. Dangers."

"Warnings!" Jamal suggested.

"Right," Alex said. "It was a kind of code."

"Yeah!" Gaby cried. "An R code!"

"In some codes you change the letters to numbers," Alex said. He loved codes, and he knew a lot about them. "In others you add extra letters to make the words look different. In this message letters in the important words were taken *out*."

"There was another weird spelling," Lenni put in. "Police R watching. Only that time the *r* wasn't missing. The rest of the word was missing."

Gaby jumped to her feet. "Danger, beware, police are watching. *That's* how the usher knew the police were coming! Whoever was running that scoreboard must have been in on the scam. We'd better call the police."

"Wait," Alex said. "There was another weird message on the scoreboard. Remember, Gaby? Right before we left. I think it was in code. Maybe if we can crack that code, we can learn something more to tell the police."

"Great," Gaby said. "Only I can't remember what the message said."

"But I bet Ghostwriter can!" Jamal said. He typed a note asking Ghostwriter to show them the last mixed-up message that had been on the electronic scoreboard.

A moment later, a message flashed onto the screen:
MRERERT ART MRORERS DRERLRI ART 12:15

All four kids stared at the screen. Then Alex grinned. "Got it," he said. "Hand me the phone, Gaby. I'm going to tell the police where they can *find* both crooks."

Can you crack the scoreboard code? Can you help the police catch the crooks? *Hint*: Find the words hidden in this shape on the next page.

A Question of Time

"That stamp's interesting," Jamal said as he leaned closer to a stamp case. "See, there's a picture of the Brooklyn Navy Yard on it."

"I like that one," Alex said, pointing to another stamp in the case. "It's from 1898. That's when Brooklyn became part of New York City."

Jamal, Alex, Lenni, and Gaby walked slowly around the small Fort Greene post office. The Stamps of Brooklyn exhibit was off to a fine start.

"Look," Gaby whispered to Alex. "Lieutenant McQuade is here."

Over in the corner the tall, burly police officer was chatting with Jamal's grandmother, Cecilia Jenkins. CeCe Jenkins worked for the postal service, and she had helped organize the exhibit. But she wasn't wear-

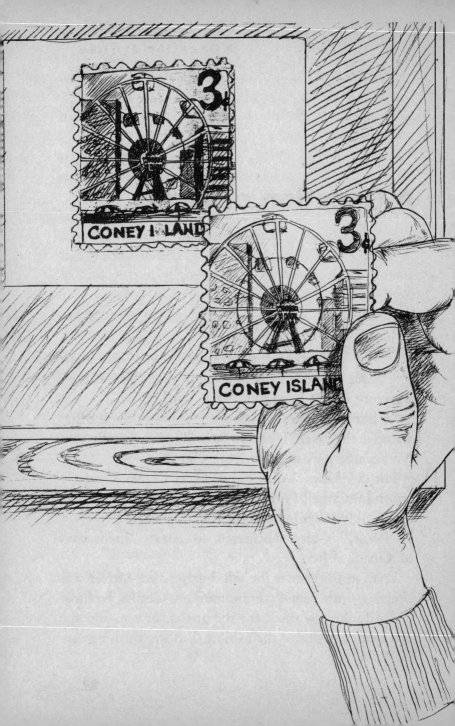

ing her blue uniform today. No deliveries, of course. It was one of her days off.

"I never knew there were so many Brooklyn stamps," Lenni said.

"Yeah," Gaby added. "It's a good thing the post office is closed today or there wouldn't be any room for the regular stamps."

Gaby and Lenni walked over to look at some stamps near the window. Gaby pointed to a stamp that was in a case by itself. "What's so special about that stamp?" she asked. "I've seen ones like it lots of times."

"So have I," Alex agreed. "I use them when I mail post cards to my pen pals abroad. Like this." He took a loose stamp out of his pocket and placed it on top of the case. Alex's stamp looked just like the rare one.

"I don't get it," Lenni said.

"Maybe Ghostwriter can figure it out," Jamal whispered. He took out a piece of paper and a pencil and wrote, "We can't figure out why the Coney Island stamp is rare."

Suddenly the letters began to scramble on the page, forming new words. Ghostwriter replied, WHY I LAND?

"Huh?" Alex said. "What does that mean?"

Gaby leaned closer to the case and studied the rare stamp. Why I land? Why I land? she thought. What did Ghostwriter mean? Then she saw what he was talking about.

"Cool!" Gaby said excitedly. "I see it. The letter *s* is missing from the word *island* on this stamp."

"*That's* what makes it rare?" Jamal asked. "A mistake?"

His grandmother had just walked up. She laughed. "It's true. The mistake is what makes that stamp rare. Only one hundred of the mistakes were printed. This is the only one that hasn't been destroyed or used."

As Grandma Jenkins spoke, the outside door opened. A cold wind blew Alex's stamp off the case. Gospel music from the church across the street drifted into the room as a thin, blond-haired woman entered.

The woman moved around the room, and Lenni noticed that she walked with a slight limp. After a few minutes she stopped by the case the team had been examining. She smiled. "How do you do," she said. "I'm Ms. Park from the Brooklyn Historical Society. I'm looking for a particular stamp. I wonder if you've seen it?"

"Could be," Jamal said. "Which one?"

"It's a Coney Island commemorative stamp."

"It's right here," Lenni said. She pointed to the case in front of her.

Ms. Park leaned over and studied the stamp carefully. "I'm *very* interested in that stamp," she said.

"Is it worth a lot of money?" Alex asked.

Ms. Park smiled again. "A great deal. Excuse me a moment." She walked across the room to the exhibit attendant, a man with a name tag that said MANUEL VEGA.

A few minutes later Ms. Park came back toward the team followed by Manuel Vega. He didn't look happy. "I can only let you see it for a minute," he was saying.

"A minute is all I need," Ms. Park replied.

Manuel opened the case and handed the Coney I land stamp to Ms. Park. She peered intently at it.

"Whoops!" Ms. Park cried all of a sudden. Gaby and Lenni gasped as the precious stamp blew out of her hand and fluttered to the floor. Immediately Gaby was on her knees, ready to pick the stamp up. But Ms. Park beat her to it.

"That was a close call, wasn't it," Ms. Park said cheerfully. She climbed to her feet and dusted off her skirt. Then she handed the stamp back to Manuel. "Thank you very much for letting me see it," she said.

While Manuel was locking up the case, Ms. Park took a train schedule out of her pocket and looked at it. It was for trains to Philadelphia, Gaby noticed. Ms. Park ran her finger down one of the columns and smiled.

A few minutes later, when Gaby looked for her again, she was gone. "I guess that Ms. Park was only here to see the Coney I land stamp," Gaby said. "She took off already."

Jamal looked at his watch. It was 2:45. "I gotta cut

out too," he said. "We have school tomorrow, and I have lots of homework."

"Yeah. We have that math test on Tuesday. That means we have only two days to study," Alex said. "And I need all the time I can get."

"I don't want to go yet, Alex," Gaby complained.

"Okay, we'll stay a couple more minutes," Alex agreed. He wasn't *that* eager to start his homework. He wished the weekend could last a little longer.

"Look at this litter," Lenni grumbled. She bent down and picked up a train schedule that was lying on the floor.

"Ms. Park must have dropped it," Gaby said.

Lenni tucked it absently into her back pocket.

"Did I just hear my name?" said a voice. Gaby turned around. A short, plump Korean woman was looking at her.

"Are you Ms. Park too?" Lenni asked.

"That's right. From the Brooklyn Historical Society," the woman answered. "I'm here about the Coney Island stamp."

Jamal laughed. "Wow. There are two of you?" he asked. "Two Ms. Parks from the Historical Society?"

"I'm the only one I know of," the new Ms. Park said.

Jamal and Lenni looked at each other. "There's something funny going on," Jamal said.

"Maybe you should talk to the attendant," Alex said to the new Ms. Park. "I'll get him."

"This is very odd," the woman said when Manuel came over. "*I'm* Ms. Park from the Historical Society. Jou-young Park. Look, here's my ID." She took a card out of her wallet and showed it to the attendant.

"Look," Alex said suddenly. "The stamp's changed!"

The team crowded around the case and stared at the rare Coney Island stamp. Alex was right. There was something different about the stamp.

"The s is back!" Gaby exclaimed.

"Oh, my goodness," the real Ms. Park said. "That isn't a rare stamp at all. It's quite common, in fact."

"Yeah. I have a whole book of them," Alex said.

"That blond lady must have taken the rare stamp!" Lenni gasped. "When she dropped it she must have switched it with that regular one."

"Oh, my goodness," the new Ms. Park said again.

"Oh, no!" cried Manuel. He looked very unhappy. "I knew I should never have taken it out of the case."

"I'll bet this was the same woman who sent me on a wild-goose chase," said the new Ms. Park. "I got a phone call this morning telling me that the exhibit had been moved to Sheepshead Bay. Sheepshead Bay is all the way at the other end of Brooklyn. The caller was a woman. Anyway, when I got to the Sheepshead Bay post office, it was closed, of course. No one was there. It took me ages to drive back here."

"I'd better call the police," Manuel said gloomily.

"Lieutenant McQuade is right over there," Jamal suggested, nodding toward the policeman.

"I'll go get him," Gaby offered. She hurried over.

"How can we find the phony Ms. Park?" Lenni asked. "She's been gone for a long time."

"Did she say where she was going, by any chance?" the real Ms. Park asked.

Lenni shook her head. "I don't think so."

Jamal took out his pad and pencil again. Whenever he needed to get his ideas clear, he took notes. For one thing, it helped him organize his thoughts. For another thing, it was a good way to keep Ghostwriter up to date on what was happening.

He wrote:

FACTS

1. Valuable Coney I land stamp has been stolen.
2. Phony Ms. Park took rare stamp. Put common one in case instead.
3. Phony Ms. Park left post office at 2:35 P.M.

Question: Where was phony Ms. Park going?

Suddenly the letters on the page rearranged themselves. 3 00P DP, wrote Ghostwriter.

Jamal gasped. "Look at this," he whispered to Lenni. He showed her his pad. "What do you think it means?"

"I don't know," Lenni whispered back.

"All right, what's this all about?" came Lieutenant McQuade's voice. He strode up to them.

Gaby was right behind him. She was about to hop up and down with excitement. "I just told you. Someone stole a stamp!" she yelped.

Then it hit Lenni. She knew what Ghostwriter meant. She snapped her fingers. "The schedule. That piece of litter I picked up—it's a train schedule!" she cried. "The phony Ms. Park is taking a train some-where!"

"Where is it?" Jamal said excitedly.

"I have it right here." Lenni yanked the schedule out of her pocket and unfolded it.

"It's a train schedule to Philadelphia," Gaby said. "So she must be on her way there."

"When?" Alex asked.

"Look," Lenni said. "There's a circle around 3:00. That must be her train. That must be what Ghostwriter meant by '3 00P DP.' That means the train departs at 3 P.M."

Jamal glanced up at the clock on the wall. It was 2:58. Too late!

"She's gone." Lenni sighed. "In two minutes that stamp will be on its way to Philadelphia."

"I liked that stamp," Gaby said sadly.

"We'll never find it now," Alex groaned.

Suddenly Jamal grabbed the train schedule from Lenni and peered at it one more time. A big grin spread over his face. "Don't be so sure," he said. "The thief made one mistake. We've still got half an hour to get that stamp back."

"What do you mean?" Lieutenant McQuade de-manded.

The lieutenant didn't have to listen to Jamal for long to understand what the stamp thief had done wrong.

New York to Philadelphia

43			◀ Train Number ▶			42
Mon-Sat			◀ Days of Operation ▶			⑫ Sun
ReadDown	Mile	▽		Symbol	▲	ReadDown
(3 00P)	0	Dp	New York, NY–Penn Sta. ● ᴱᵀ	Ⓢ	Dp	3 30P
R 3 13P	10		Newark, NJ ⑫	Ⓢ &		D 3 44P
3 27P	25		Metropark, NJ	& ㉛		4 00P
3 37P	33		New Brunswick, NJ	⊘ ㉛		4 10P
3 51P	49		Princeton Jct., NJ (㉚)	⊘ & ㉛		4 26P
4 01P	58		Trenton, NJ	Ⓢ &		4 38P
4 14P	86	▼	North Philadelphia, PA	⊘	▼	4 54P
4 25P	91	Ar	Philadelphia, PA ⑨ ◎	Ⓢ &	Ar	5 05P

In five minutes he was out the door and on his way to Penn Station.

That night Jamal was doing his homework when the phone rang. A moment later his mother came into his room. "It's for you, sugar pie," she told him. "It's Lieutenant McQuade."

Jamal went to the phone and picked it up.

"Hello, Jamal. Well done," said Lieutenant McQuade.

"Did you catch the lady who stole the stamp?" Jamal asked.

"We sure did," Lieutenant McQuade told him. "She was right where you said she'd be. At the station, waiting for her train. Thanks, son. We couldn't have done it without you and your friends."

Jamal hung up the phone. Then he turned on his computer and wrote a note telling Ghostwriter everything Lt. McQuade had said. He asked Ghostwriter to carry the note to the rest of the team.

I WONDER IF LIEUTENANT MCQUADE WOULD HAVE FIGURED IT OUT BY HIMSELF, Jamal added.

I THINK SO, Ghostwriter wrote back. IT WAS JUST A QUESTION OF TIME!

How did Jamal know that the woman with the stamp would still be at the station? It was a question of time and *days*. To follow Jamal's reasoning, figure out what day it is in the story. Read the sentences below. Some

A Question of Time

of them contain important clues that will help you figure out the day of the week. Some sentences are "red herrings." Red herrings are details that seem important but don't really matter. Can you pick out the important details and figure out what mistake the stamp thief made?

1. "We have that math test on Tuesday. That means we have only two days to study," Alex said.
2. The woman moved around the room, and Lenni noticed that she walked with a slight limp.
3. "It's a good thing the post office is closed today or there wouldn't be any room for the regular stamps," Gaby said.
4. "Sheepshead Bay is all the way at the other end of Brooklyn," the new Ms. Park said.
5. Gospel music from the church across the street drifted into the room as a thin, blond-haired woman entered.

Hint: When you know what day it is go back and study the train schedule carefully.

The Polar Bear Puzzle

"This is it. This is it!" Gaby Fernandez shouted. "It's my chance. Stardom is mine at last."

Alex Fernandez looked up from his book. "Slow down, Gaby," he said. "What are you talking about?"

It was a quiet summer day in the Fernandezes' small grocery store. Alex and Gaby were working behind the counter, but there weren't many customers. Ivan Bowman, the new stockboy, whistled as he stacked mangoes and plantains on the fruit stand outside.

Gaby held up her newspaper. "'Art wanted,'" she read. "'Calling all artists: Join a community art contest for immigrant Americans. The winner will receive a cash prize and appear on television with his or her artwork.'"

Alex shrugged his shoulders. "So?"

"What do you mean, ' so'?" Gaby said, waving her arms. "Don't you get it? We could be on TV!"

"How? We're not artists," Alex pointed out. "And we're not immigrants, either. Mom and Dad are, but you and I were born here in the States."

"No, no," Gaby said impatiently. "I'm talking about that big . . . that big *thing* across the street."

"The polar bear?" Alex asked.

A week ago a huge statue had appeared in the park across the street from their store. No one knew who had donated it. No one had even seen it arrive. One day it was just there. It was made of milky-white stone. Alex thought it looked like a big polar bear.

"Right," Gaby replied. "We could enter it in the contest. And if it won, then we'd be on TV." She poked Alex in the ribs. "It's our big chance!"

Ivan came inside. He was a tall, very skinny black teenager with a squared-off haircut. He disappeared silently into the stockroom.

"So what about it, Alex?" Gaby asked.

"Gaby, we can't enter the contest," Alex told his sister. "The person who made it would have to enter it. And then *that* person would be on TV. Not us."

"If they tape the statue, we could be hanging around, couldn't we? You know, in the background. After all, it is right across the street from our bodega."

Alex thought about that. Finally he said, "I guess so." It would be great to be on TV, he thought. Then something else occurred to him. "But we don't know who the artist is."

"Who *what* artist is?" asked a voice. The voice had a thick Russian accent, and it belonged to a tall, heavy-set woman with iron-gray hair.

"Hi, Mrs. Radchenko!" Gaby smiled at her. Mrs. Radchenko and her husband owned a furniture store on DeKalb Avenue. "We're talking about the artist who made that big white statue," Gaby explained. "Do you know who did it?"

"No, I don't," Mrs. Radchenko said. "But whoever the artist is, he has verrry grrreat talent." She rolled her *r*s when she said "very" and "great." She turned to a plump man with round glasses who was behind her. "Do you agree, Mr. Masoud?"

"Hmm." Behind his glasses Mr. Masoud's eyes were soft and brown. "I don't really know," he said. "It just looks like a lump of rock to me."

"But do you know who made it?" Alex asked.

"I'm afraid not," Mr. Masoud admitted.

Ivan came back out of the stockroom with a crate of oranges. He carried them outside without saying a word.

"That boy is very quiet," Mrs. Radchenko said.

It was true, Ivan didn't talk much. He was seventeen—five years older than Alex—and he was very shy. He was new in the neighborhood. He had just moved to New York from Rhode Island and lived with his grandparents. He was going to college in the fall. Alex and Gaby didn't know anything else about him except that he liked to stack the fruits on the stands in interesting shapes.

"How can we find out who made the statue?" Gaby asked after Mrs. Radchenko and Mr. Masoud left.

Alex shrugged. "Somebody must know. We should ask around," he said.

"Okay. But we have to hurry." Gaby looked at her newspaper again. Then she let out a little gasp. "And I mean hurry! The contest deadline is tomorrow!"

After that, every time someone came up to the counter, Alex or Gaby would ask if he or she knew who had made the white sculpture. Everyone had something to say about it. Some people liked it. Others thought it was ugly. But no one knew the name of the artist who had made it.

Finally Jamal stopped by. He had a basketball under his arm. "Want to play some hoop?" he asked Alex.

"Can't, I'm working. Hey, we have a problem," Alex said. He told Jamal about Gaby's idea. "It's weird. No one knows where the statue came from or who made it."

"We're stuck," Gaby added glumly.

Jamal looked interested. "How else could we find out? I mean, besides just asking around?"

Gaby looked around to make sure no one else could hear. "Let's ask Ghostwriter," she whispered. "He might help."

Jamal nodded. "Let's do it," he said.

Gaby grabbed a pen and a pad and wrote: DEAR GHOSTWRITER, WE ARE TRYING TO FIND OUT THE NAME OF AN ARTIST SO THAT WE CAN ENTER HIS SCULPTURE IN A CONTEST. NO ONE KNOWS WHO HE IS. CAN YOU HELP?

She put down the pen. The three kids waited eagerly.

A second later the letters in Gaby's note scrambled into a new message. It said: CHECK SCULPTURE FOR NAME. MOST ARTISTS SIGN WORK.

Gaby sat back with a huge grin on her face. "I knew he'd know what to do," she said. "Ghostwriter is so cool."

As soon as Gaby and Alex finished working at the bodega, the team raced outside. By that time Lenni and Tina had come by too and heard about the mystery of the white statue.

All five kids ran across the street to the tiny park. The statue sat in the middle of it. "It looks like a snowy mountain," Lenni said.

"I think it looks like a polar bear," Alex told her. That made him think. "Maybe what the sculpture looks like will tell us who made it," he said. "I mean, let's say it *is* a polar bear. Who would make a statue of a polar bear?"

"An Eskimo!" Gaby cried.

Tina shook her head impatiently. "How many Eskimos do you know who live in Brooklyn?" she asked.

"None," Lenni said. "At least, none in this neighborhood."

"It doesn't have to be an Eskimo," Alex said. "Other people live where there are polar bears too."

"Some parts of Russia go way up, almost to the North Pole," Jamal put in.

"Yeah!" Alex cried. He was excited now. "And we have Russians right in our own neighborhood. The Radchenkos."

"My dad says they came to this country from Siberia," Lenni said. "So they're immigrants. And Siberia is a cold, snowy part of Russia. There might be polar bears there."

Alex thought about Mr. and Mrs. Radchenko. They were both big people. They looked kind of like friendly bears themselves. He could just picture them, carving the white statue and then putting it in the park. It probably reminded them of home. "I bet they made the statue," he said.

"Maybe," Tina said. She looked doubtful.

"Well, let's look for the artist's name. It's the only way we'll find out for sure," Lenni said.

The team began to examine the white statue. Lenni, Jamal, and Tina looked near its base. Alex scanned the middle part, the part he thought of as the bear's belly. Gaby climbed onto the sculpture and looked around its top.

She ran her fingers over the stone. It was smooth and cool. There were no sharp edges anywhere. And no writing.

"There's nothing down here that looks like a signature," Tina called. "Did you find anything up there?"

"Nope," Gaby called back. "But it's gotta be here."

"Hey!" Jamal shouted suddenly. "I found something."

Everybody crowded around him. He was peering into a little hollow on one of the bear's legs. "There's something scratched in the stone here," he said. "I can feel the marks. But I can't see what it says."

"Make a rubbing," Lenni said. She pulled a notebook from her back pocket. "Anyone got a pencil?"

Alex had one. Jamal took the pencil and a sheet of paper. He fitted the paper into the hollow in the statue. Then he gently rubbed the pencil point over the paper.

A minute later he smoothed out the piece of paper and laid it on the ground. The places where the stone was scratched showed up as white spaces on the gray paper.

"Let me see!" Gaby cried. She leaned over Jamal's shoulder and stared at the paper. Whose name was on it?

"Huh?" she said after a second. The markings on the paper weren't letters at all. They were pictures. They looked like this:

"An eye, a box, a bow—or is that a butterfly? And a man," Tina said. "What does it mean?"

"Nothing," Alex said. He was very disappointed.

"It must mean something," Lenni insisted.

Jamal had been studying the drawings. Now he said, "You know, not all languages use the same letters we use. Some use pictures instead."

"You mean like Chinese?" Tina piped up. "These don't look like Chinese characters to me."

Jamal frowned. "I was thinking . . . the Egyptians used to use picture writing. I forget what they called it."

"Glyphs!" Gaby shouted. "Egyptian letters are called glyphs. Nice going, Jamal. These drawings are glyphs!"

"Hold on a second, Gaby," Lenni said. "Are you sure?"

"Have you ever seen a glyph?" Tina added.

"Well, no," Gaby admitted. She folded her arms. "But what else could these be? They must be glyphs."

"And get this," Jamal said suddenly. "There's an Egyptian in the neighborhood. Mr. Masoud!"

"But Mr. Masoud was in the bodega this afternoon and he said he didn't even like the polar bear," Alex said.

"He was covering up," Gaby said instantly.

Alex rolled his eyes. "What for? And besides, why would an Egyptian person make a statue of a polar bear?"

"How do we know it's really a polar bear?" Jamal replied. "That's just what it looks like to you."

"Come on, Alex. Mr. Masoud did it," Gaby argued. "It had to be him. He lives in America, but he was born in another country. He's perfect for the contest!"

"But we have no proof he's an artist," Alex said.

"We don't have any proof about the Radchenkos, either," Lenni pointed out.

"Proof or no proof, I have to go home for dinner," Tina said, looking at her watch. "See you guys tomorrow."

"Get up early," Gaby yelled after her. "If we miss the contest deadline, that'll be a real disaster!"

The next morning Lenni went over to Jamal's house. He was up in his room and was surrounded by library books. "These are books about Egypt," he told her. "To help us figure out what the glyphs mean."

"If they're really glyphs," Lenni reminded him.

"They've gotta be," Jamal said. He opened one of the books and pointed to a drawing of an eye. "Look, that glyph is the same as the eye that's carved on the statue."

Lenni peered at the eye glyph. Then she looked at the rubbing Jamal had taken from the statue. "Are you sure?"

"Come on, Lenni," Jamal said. "An eye is an eye."

"I guess you're right. Well, let's get started," Lenni said. She picked up one of the books and started reading.

Half an hour later Jamal closed his book. "I'm not doing very well," he admitted. "I found a glyph that looks like an eye, and another one that looks like the man here, but I can't find that funny-looking box or the ribbon."

"Me neither," Lenni said. "Do you think Ghostwriter could help? He's a faster reader than I am."

"Let's ask," Jamal said. He sat down at his computer and typed, GHOSTWRITER, CAN YOU READ EGYPTIAN GLYPHS?

The screen was blank for a moment. Then Ghostwriter's reply appeared: I CAN TRY. GLYPHS ARE A TYPE OF WRITTEN WORDS. WHERE ARE THEY?

"IN THESE BOOKS," Jamal typed. "LOOK IN

THE BOOKS FOR GLYPHS THAT MATCH THE ONES ON THE GRAY PIECE OF PAPER."

There was a long pause. Then Ghostwriter asked, MATCH WHAT? I CAN'T FIND A GRAY PIECE OF PAPER.

Lenni frowned. "It's right here," she said. "Tell Ghostwriter it's next to the computer, Jamal."

Jamal started to type again. But then, suddenly, his fingers froze. He turned and stared at Lenni. "That's it!" he yelled. "Ghostwriter just told us the answer!"

"What are you talking about?" Lenni asked.

"Ghostwriter can't find the gray piece of paper *because there are no words on it*! Ghostwriter can only see letters and words. Glyphs can stand for words, but those drawings aren't glyphs at all," Jamal said. "They're pictures! Just plain pictures. We've been looking at them all wrong."

"What are you talking about?" Lenni asked.

"I'll explain later." Jamal turned and typed RALLY AT STATUE. A second later the words vanished. Ghostwriter was off to find the team.

Ten minutes later Alex, Gaby, and Tina met Lenni and Jamal at the big white statue. Across the street they could see Ivan arranging peaches into tall piles.

Jamal didn't waste any time. "We checked out some books on glyphs, and I don't think the pictures carved on the statue are glyphs at all," he said. "I think they're meant to be a rebus. You know, the kind of puzzle where the pictures stand for different sounds. When you put the sounds together, you get words."

"Oh, I see!" Tina cried. "So the picture of the eye here stands for the sound I."

"Yeah. And the picture of the man stands for the word *man*," Lenni said.

"Yeah, but what about that weird box?" Alex said. "What sound does that stand for? Ibox? That's not a word."

"Maybe it's not a box," Jamal said. "What else could it be?"

The team crowded around. They studied the piece of paper with the drawings on it.

Then Gaby slapped her forehead. "I don't believe it," she groaned. "There goes my chance to be a TV star."

"What do you mean?" Tina asked.

"I know who the artist is," Gaby said. "The answer was right under our noses all this time. We just never looked at the big picture!"

Who is the mysterious artist, and how did Gaby figure it out?

Gaby made up her own rebus to show what she knows. Look at the rebus and see if you can solve it. Fill in the sounds in the blanks below each drawing. Then put the sounds together to read the message! *Hint:* Use the key to solve the rebus name in the story.

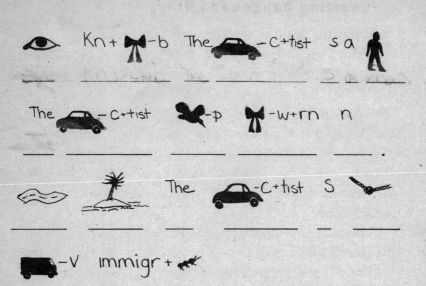

Key:
- = car
- = wasp
- = road
- = island
- = man
- = knot
- = van
- = ant
- = bow
- = eye

Answers

Photo Finish: The word that's not in the word search is *does*. Does are female deer. Henry, the middle runner, is red-handed AND has the word "does" on his T-shirt.

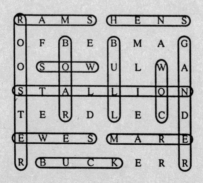

Courting Danger: The hidden message is *Meet at Moe's Deli at 12:15.*

To find it: The hint hidden inside the balloons says *Leave out every R.* Cross out all the *r*s in the mixed-up scoreboard message. You'll see the crook's real message in no time!

A Question of Time: The thief forgot it was Sunday. The train she circled is a train that only runs on *weekdays.* The Sunday train doesn't leave until 3:30 in the afternoon.

The red herring sentences are 2 and 4. All the other sentences tell you that it's Sunday.

The Polar Bear Puzzle: The artist is Ivan Bowman. Gaby's rebus message says: *I know the artist is a man. The artist was born in Rhode Island. The artist is not an immigrant.*